Foundation to Fi

A Soul Constructional

Tara T Tate

Illustrations by Carissa Newkirk

ISBN: 978-1-963919-51-6

Dedication

To Ma, Grandma, and Colet

Acknowledgment

The word beauty can bring all sorts of images to mind. Most people think of something that fits a popular version of beauty, like someone with beautiful clothes, beautiful makeup, hair, or even the beauty of an animal or other art pieces. But how many of us really think about how God describes beauty?

In the Bible, God references beauty many times as being an internal quality. God looks at inward beauty, not what our appearance is to the world. 1 Peter 1:22 talks about "purifying your souls by obeying the truth." When we decide to be obedient to God, this purifies our souls, which is the inner beauty that is so lovingly referred to. In her book Foundation to Finishing, Tara covers the scriptures that define what God believes beauty to be,

Miss Tara Tate is certified as a Christian Health Mentor with WBW (Women Becoming Whole) as well as having a ROKU channel, gloWhole Inward Repair, Outward Result. Tara's unshakable faith has stemmed from being shown through life there is a Creator. She has shaped her life by the Holy Spirit. She was inspired to write this book due to the pressure that is put on people concerning their outward beauty. Tara hopes to inspire people to be happy with themselves as the Creator intended, with all people being beautiful as the Creator believes them to be.

I have known Tara now for over two years. She lives what she talks about, inspiring people to be the best they can, as we all are beautiful in the eyes of the Creator. She has inspired me to pick up the pen again, and finish my own story of events that documents the amazing things the Creator has done for us! My own story of hope and inspiration started out with my 10 year old son being diagnosed with AML leukemia, but today he is over 14 years in remission! I hope to be able to spread hope to those going through a similar situation, as I know Tara has inspired others with her own story!

Happy reading!

Stacey A Crowder

Contents

About the Author

The author created a website that started as a blog but has become a lifestyle of living on purpose in purpose. It was her display of loving herself and others because of the Love given to us by God. It became a celebration of the uniqueness! This led to the logo, Rara T. Avis, an eagle with butterfly wings in the color of royalty; blue and purple. The expansion continued with a podcast. Each podcast episode was paired with a playlist curated by the author. All of these platforms display that the author is multifaceted and is not ashamed to explore each facet with enthusiasm without shame.

The start of the journey into my purpose started with the poetry at the end of this book. Long Talk Little Walk, copyright 2006, is a collection of poetry created at the beginning of wisdom.

Preface

No amount of foundation, blush, lipstick or eyeshadow can mask a damaged soul. The glow that comes from the depths of a healed psyche cannot be duplicated. Just like facial makeup regiments are individualized depending on skin type, skin hue, sensitivities, and imperfections so are soul makeovers.

However, there are basics that lead everyone to healing the innermost parts of ourselves so that the best of us comes shining through. Makeup is advertised to erase or minimize skin imperfections by people who usually do not have any skin imperfections. But that is not the intriguing part. The intriguing part is that you will rarely hear any backlash about a commercial claiming to make your skin perfect. Yet there are preachers of the Gospel who will create entire sermons about not being able to become perfect.

Wait. Preachers. Of the Gospel. Have a problem with a Believer saying we can become perfect because the Creator of the universe says that we can and gives us the means by which to do it. But these same preachers of the Gospel do not have a problem with a product made by imperfect people claiming to make your appearance perfect. And no one appears to have a problem with it.

Immediately rebuttals appear. "How can you say that?" "What's your proof?" The proof is in the Holy Glamour Pinups featured on programs, websites, flyers, and posters whenever there is a conference, gathering, or prayer meeting happening. Preachers have a problem saying believers can be perfect by the Spirit of the Highest God but have no issue with the pounds of makeup used to hawk these perfect facades. I'm not just talking about the women who preach the Gospel. Men wear makeup too. If that does not disturb your sensibilities more than being perfect as Christ is perfect then no wonder the world is facing the ills of mental wellness.

Man looks at the outward and God looks at the heart. Correct me please if you must. But with that statement would it not be logical, wise, and intelligent to believe that people after God's own heart would follow that same example for a dying world to view? When Daniel and the three Hebrew boys turned down the King's food to fast before their God, they put up a challenge about their countenance being better than those who feasted on the delights of the king because they would be in the presence of the True King. The Perfect King.

It baffles me to see so much social media space and streaming video space devoted to self-care when knowing thyself is never in the forefront. Self-care is patterned after people who look perfect so it is assumed that what they are preaching is so much better than the God who created you. "If I get this pedicure, massage, or smoothie I will have mental wellness and wholeness."

How is that working?

Please do not misunderstand my intention. I have not come to abolish your makeup, self-care Sunday, or your healthcare routine. I am asking you to take care of the part of you that is often neglected and overlooked because the average person cannot see it. The part of you that makeup cannot disguise or perfect. The part of you once healed will cause you to glow from within. Once we heal this part of you, the cares of this world fade away. The cares are fueled by the lust of the eyes, the lust of the flesh, and the pride of life.

Once the soul is given a makeover the most important things are your focus. Pettiness and competitiveness are washed away like so much dross because once you tap into the core of who you are the beauty of the divine created by God can finally shine.

The Blueprint is in the Word

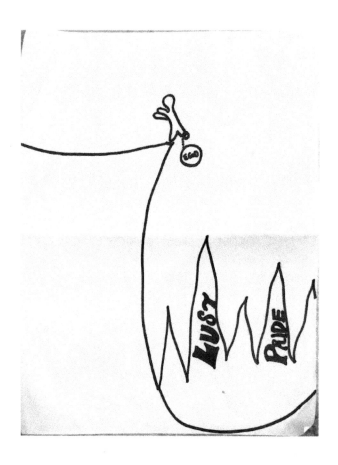

I Corinthians 15:45 says that God created Adam a soul. God gave Adam dominion over all things. So, it was by God's sovereign authority that Adam had dominion.

He then placed Adam with his wife in the Garden of Eden. Telling Adam that he may freely eat of all things except one tree. Eve was tempted by the serpent to eat from the forbidden tree.

Since Eve offered the forbidden fruit to Adam they were put out of the Garden for their own good. They chose to eat from the tree of death which God in His Love and Grace did not want them to live eternally in that mindset. So, he put them away from the Tree of Life.

We have the same choice as Adam, a soul created by God, even though we are born into sin. Our choice is offered through the perfect sacrifice of Christ. Christ is the only begotten of the Father and a life-giving spirit.

Now, we have the option to either choose death by not accepting the offer of life from the tree that Christ died upon. Christ died on the tree yet conquered the grave to obtain the keys of death and hell.

Christ instructs us to take His yoke upon us because it is light. His burden easy. His Love will not force it on us. The same as God the Father did not forcibly prohibit Adam from eating from the tree of Knowledge of good and evil.

The Father could have programmed the soul of Adam to do only what He wished. Yet that is not the heart of our Father.

God the Father created the soul of Adam and then showered His Love upon him. The Love of the Father was shown by the dominion He gave Adam, the helper he provided Adam, and the perfect dwelling and provision. All that the father offered was light and easy. However, the soul of the man Adam could not appreciate it.

Therefore, the Father sent Himself as redeemer for all of mankind, in the flesh of a human. The redemption offers eternal life in His presence. Shall we say the soul seeks that which does not satisfy or sustain life? The soul is the basest portion of a being. The soul pleasures in the desires that are temporal.

God created humans to make a conscious decision and effort to choose life. Eternal life. When given the choicest provision of all God had to offer, Adam the soul, chose to disobey God.

In all of His loving Grace God asked the soul, Adam to choose Him. God is illustrating the struggle we all have, conditioning our uttermost foundational part to choose to obey Him.

This simple fact is made complicated by the lust of the flesh, the pride of life, and the lust of the eyes as I John 2:16 states. This scripture illustrates that humans have the same foe we have had since Adam and Eve were in the Garden. However, we know not to make the same mistake Adam made. We must realize that it is our responsibility to make an account for our souls. We must be consciously aware of the soul's existence and the soul's desires.

The constructional you are about to read explores scripture's treatise of the soul.

Section I: The Foundation is General

Psalm 49:15

But God will redeem my soul from the power of the grave,

For He shall receive me. Selah

God has all power and authority. God the Father gave the Son the opportunity to take power over hell, death, and the grave when He sent Christ to earth and offered Him as a sacrifice—a sacrifice for our soul.

When Christ arose on the third day, He arose with all power and authority over our foe. We must realize that God could have made the world just as He wanted without hell. Adam was never told about death until God impressed upon him the importance of making the right choice to nourish himself.

God would have preferred that Adam would have never eaten from the Tree of Knowledge of good and evil. But God, because of His love, made The Way to redeem the disobedient soul.

As I speak of death, I would take this opportunity to discuss the significance of my logo, Rara T. Avis. It is comprised of two beings that must choose life. The eagle is given the opportunity to live a second portion of life or die. If the eagle chooses to live, then it must get rid of a useless beak by beating it against a rock and stripping away matted feathers. Both of these acts are to produce newness.

And we all know about the caterpillar transforming into a butterfly in a cocoon. The wings of the butterfly are strengthened as it fights to be free of the cocoon. What if the butterfly decides not to fight? Surely, it will die in the place which was to serve as its rebirth.

I Peter 1:22

Since you have purified your souls in obeying the truth through the Spirit in sincere love of the brethren, love one another fervently with a pure heart.

This scripture makes it clear that disobedience is a choice that we make, which purifies our souls. How did my soul get dirty, you ask? Our soul is made dirty from birth because all humans after Adam were born into sin.

The choice that Adam made to eat from the Tree of the Knowledge of Good and Evil was a choice made for all mankind. Eve was named such by Adam because she was the mother of all living, as stated in Genesis 3:20.

Eve is the mother of the soul. She ate from the tree of knowledge of good and evil because Genesis 3:6 says the same that is said in I John. She saw (with eyes of lust) that it was good to eat from, and the pride of life made her see that the tree was desirable to make one wise. The choice that Eve made causes us to be born into sin.

After we reach the age of consent, we must choose to accept the sacrifice of the Spirit Son, Christ. At such time that we receive Christ, we must make a conscious effort to become obedient to God and purify our souls. This is the only way that we can live out the most important commandments:

To love the Lord our God with all our heart

To love our neighbor as ourselves

It is apparent that we must first love ourselves to purify ourselves. It is a sincere love because it must deny the lust of the flesh, the pride of life, and the lust of the eyes.

Corinthians 15:45

And so, it is written, "The first man Adam became a living being." The last Adam became a life-giving spirit.

The scripture above says Adam became a living soul and the last Adam, Christ, became a life-giving spirit. Even if Adam had good intentions, God did not imbue Adam with the power to cleanse our souls. God the Father discussed Adam with Christ, not the other way around. When Adam and Eve were put out of the Garden, it was established by the triune council of the Father, Son, and Holy Spirit.

Psalm 103:1

Bless the Lord, O my soul;

And all that is within me, bless His holy name!

This is a command to the soul. The soul must be told what to do by the mind. The mind is the organ that makes the decisions. The soul must obey what the mind dictates. Therefore, the mind must be solely stayed on Christ for the soul to obey and choose life continually.

If the mind waffles between two opinions, then what choice does the soul have but to waffle as well? The psalm goes on to say, "And all that is within me." The soul is the seat of the manifestation of action. The soul is told to bless the LORD and then all other occupants of the vessel fall in line to bless His holy name.

It's as if the mind is issuing a wake-up call to the nether regions of the being that are not always engaged in the daily activities. Instead of the words "wake up," the mind is saying "bless the LORD" and then specifies whom it is talking to.

This reminds me of the story of Lazarus. Our LORD called Lazarus forth from death by first specifying whom He was talking to so that everyone in the grave would not come forth. Here the mind, the Head of the body of Christ, Christ himself is giving the command which all souls must respond. Therefore, the mind of the actual body is giving the command because it wants the entire body to respond to the command: Bless the LORD! (Wake UP!)

Psalm 103:2

Bless the Lord, O my soul,

And forget not all His benefits:

We continue to witness the mind commanding the soul: "And forget none of His benefits." As I discussed earlier, the soul is the seat of the basest desires. So, the mind is reminding the soul of all the LORD offers.

Adam could have done well to have that reminder in the Garden. "Before you partake, Adam, from the fruit of the forbidden tree, do you recall everything else that you have access to? Perhaps this command would have been a good constructional to himself every morning. 'Good morning, self' (which included his partner because they were not yet separate), 'forget not all of the LORD's benefits before you go about your day. Meditate on the goodness of our God who has provided for us all that is needed for fulfillment and wholeness. Take a look around, could it get any better than this?'"

This instruction is a few centuries too late for Adam but spot on for us. Bless the LORD, O my soul. And forget not His benefits. Tara's soul, listen up: look at your provision, your health, your joy, your love, your freedom—this list could go on endlessly since the command is to not forget any of His benefits.

I have no groundbreaking revelation from this passage. Just an age-old reminder: when you are listing your blessings, you have no time to grumble about any lack or ill wind. One guess of who is drawn to that atmosphere: the Spirit of the One True God.

Once this constructional is made into a practice, guess who dwells in your habitations no matter where the habitation is located. Remember and at midnight Paul and Silas prayed and sang praises (Acts 16:25-34). Is it any large leap to understand that the prisoners were set free by the Spirit of the Living God? There is a silent command of Paul that the scriptures did not print: "Bless the LORD, O my soul."

Jeremiah 31:14

I will satiate the soul of the priests with abundance,

And My people shall be satisfied with My goodness, says the Lord.

God decrees He will fill the soul of the Levites, the tribe of the priesthood, with abundance. The Levites were those who did not worship the Golden Calf when Aaron was left in charge of a rebellious restless, complaining group of Israelites.

The Levites had distinguished themselves as ones who would not be pacified by any other God. The hunger and thirst of the Levites was for that which only God could give them. Notice God is not stingy with the delivery. He fills the soul of the Levites with abundance. Remember, the soul is the seat of desire and lust, an insatiable container. The promise of God to fill this container is extraordinary from that fact alone.

However, He goes on to say, "My people will be satisfied with My goodness." Not only will the Levites have more than enough for their soul to swim in, but that abundance will satisfy God's people too. There is no way to review this topic without discussing what the priests are thirsting for even in present-day times.

Let's make the Golden Calf "social justice," "racial equality," or "gender equality." The true lovers of God are not distracted by what does not satisfy. The Golden Calf was an event for a moment but it would not fulfill the missing element: Fellowship with God.

Aaron got fed up with their complaining and gave the multitude what the seat of their desire and lust asked for—an idol to worship, an outlet for their unholy desires. Yet in the midst of this, there was a remnant who knew in their hearts and minds the One True God. And their soul would not be satisfied with anything less.

The Levites' containers were pure and holy so that which came out would be the same. Instead of spouting blasphemy about the goodness of the Golden Calf, they held out for true satisfaction—a God deposit, the deposit that fills every void.

Psalm 107:9

For He satisfies the longing soul,

And fills the hungry soul with goodness.

How wonderful it is to know you are being filled with what is good. The only good and perfect filling comes from God. Only the soul that has chosen God can appreciate the goodness of the filling.

Just as we discussed with the Levites, the Levites could not be satisfied even a little by a worthless idol. Isaiah 55:2 says, "Why do you spend your money for that which is not bread and your labor for that which does not satisfy? Listen carefully to Me, and eat what is good, and your soul will delight in the richest of foods." This verse was presented in Isaiah; however, could God be speaking to Adam, Eve, or me as well?

The things and ways of God are an acquired taste. It is rare that someone eating potted meat today is going to crave the choicest cut of lamb tomorrow. The taste for the choice cuts of meat is cultivated over time and experience. This cultivated appetite is not something that someone can be dragged to and forced to enjoy. Either one wants it for themselves by a hunger and thirst that desires God or else it will hunger and thirst for the lust of the eyes, lust of the flesh, and the pride of life.

God fills us with what is good. Do you notice that when you fill your earthly body with good foods—choice cuts of meat, fresh fruits and vegetables, pure produce, and dairy—if you deviate from this regimen, your body reacts noticeably? The same is true for our souls.

God admonished Adam to feed himself from the choicest of vegetation. Make it a habit, Adam; then you won't have to worry about craving what I instructed you not to eat. Be filled, Adam, with what is good that I am providing for you.

Hebrews 10:39

But we are not of those who draw back to perdition, but of those who believe in the saving of the soul.

The brethren are being asked to continue cultivating the hunger and thirst for the things of God. Do not shrink back to wanting the lusts and pride of worldly life, but preserve your soul by hungering and thirsting for good things.

Interestingly, destruction is linked to not preserving the soul. Destruction means complete and utter ruin or damage beyond repair. Christ came to offer wholeness and completeness in Him and His sacrifice. By rejecting what Christ offered, in the same manner that Adam rejected God's offer of eternal life, the only option is death.

Also, preserving the soul is a forward and active motion. One cannot preserve the soul in one definitive action. It is an ongoing practice that is done at all times, just like nurturing a garden. A garden is not kept by a once-and-for-all action. A garden has many activities that must continually take place for it to prosper. It must be plowed, planted, watered, weeded, and harvested to be well-kept. The same is true of our souls.

Even despite all the activities to prosper the garden, faith is still needed. This faith does not lie in our works but in the One who came, died, and rose to grant us salvation. Faith that He will and does keep His promises. No matter what our eyes see, we must have faith that our souls have been redeemed. Without this faith, then we may as well feed our flesh, eyes, and worldly desires.

The believers' walk is onward and upward, never back to what we were delivered from when Christ found us.

Hebrews 6:19

This hopes we have as an anchor of the soul, both sure and steadfast, and which enters the Presence behind the veil,

One of my favorite quotes is, "All who wander are not lost." And the best visual expression I have seen of that is a tote bag from Cracker Barrel that has a picture of an untethered anchor. It has a rope tied to the anchor, yet the rope is not tied to anything.

This is the way I feel being anchored to the LORD. The hope we have by believing that God is who He says He is. His promise to His children is that He is the anchor for our souls. So first, our mind must believe within our hearts that God exists. Once this happens, our souls are free to experience the freedom, peace, and power that lies behind the veil.

If there was not something spectacular behind the veil, it wouldn't have been a central theme throughout the scriptures. In the Old Testament, one could not venture beyond the veil without the threat of death if they were not pure. This imagery is much like the Garden. Once Adam and Eve were banished from the Garden, God placed a flaming sword to guard the entrance, protected by cherubim. Needless to say, Adam and Eve could not just waltz back into the Garden without consequences, much like going beyond the veil for the Israelites if they were not pure.

But God, in the literal Grace of His Son Christ, tore the veil after Christ's sacrifice for redemption. Almost as if giving all mankind after Christ access to dwell with God in the Garden anytime they chose. As in the days when the "soul" Adam was free to communicate with God face to face. Free to be nurtured by and taught by God without distraction by the lust of the flesh, the pride of life, and the lust of the eyes.

Ezekiel 18:4

"Behold, all souls are Mine;

The soul of the father

As well as the soul of the son is Mine;

The soul who sins shall die.

Consider the previous passage when reading this one from Ezekiel. Behold, all souls are Mine. Adam belonged to God. So, what allowed the stealing away? Adam's choice through free will allowed the appearance of being stolen away from God.

The lesson here is that choices have consequences. Adam's choice to disobey God had consequences of death, toil, labor, as well as pain. God told Adam that when he ate from the Tree of the Knowledge of good and evil he would surely die. God repeats that admonishment here in Ezekiel 18:4, "The soul who sins will die". Sin is defined as doing anything against God's will.

The fact is clearly seen with Adam and Eve. God's will for Adam to live by the Spirit. God admonished Adam to eat from the Tree of Life. Life in the Garden in communication with Him was God's will. However, since Adam had free will he could choose to eat from any tree in the Garden including the one that God instructed him not to eat.

Adam had perfect knowledge of God's will and still disobeyed it. Clearly sin. Surely Adam died the moment he disobeyed God. The punishment for sin is death. God does not change therefore that precept did not change. Yet God in His mercy sent Christ to conquer death in His sacrifice on the cross.

The passage in Ezekiel makes clear to whom all souls belong. The Omnipotent and the Omniscient One. The One who knows the choices of every being on earth as well as above and below. Therefore, He declares that the soul who sins will die. He knew before the foundation of the universe the souls that would choose Him. And because He owns all souls, He decides the fate of each one according to their own choice.

James 5:20

Let him know that he who turns a sinner from the error of his way will save a soul from death and cover a multitude of sins.

This scripture solidifies the precept that sin is death and the sinner has a choice. There would be no reason for God to tell us to turn a sinner from the error of his way if the sinner did not have the power to choose not to sin. God is a just God. Therefore, God would not decree a thing that could not be done.

The verse before this says that the one who is being turned is the one who has wandered from the Truth. Would an entire species have been born into sin if Adam had brought the one who was drawn out of him back to the knowledge of the Truth? I have no idea the answer to that question. However, God did not have to wonder because He already knew the choice Adam would make. A just and merciful God had already made provision for Adam's choice.

Consider for a moment that Adam would have turned Eve back to the knowledge of the Truth, the Word of God, and then her sin would have been covered. Yet as it stands, they were both left trying to cover their disobedience by their own means which was fruitless in the presence of the Almighty.

I Peter 1:9

Receiving the end of your faith—the salvation of your souls.

Scripture says that faith is the substance of things hoped for and the evidence of things not seen in Hebrews 11:1. The passage of scripture above from I Peter discusses how the faith of those who have not seen God obtains salvation for our souls.

How much easier was it for Christ's disciples to believe after He presented Himself to them? Many had seen Him crucified, and the others had definitely heard the report. So, when He appeared on the road to Emmaus and in the midst of their gatherings, the disciples had physical proof of their belief in the Messiah.

Those of us coming after must have faith that the scriptures are true. This faith obtains wholeness for our souls. Not only in That Great and Awful Day but every day of our lives we believe, faith is power. The belief in the Gospel of Jesus Christ is the power unto Salvation. Wonder-working power each and every day of our lives until That Great and Awful Day arrives.

Psalm 49:8

For the redemption of their souls is costly,

And it shall cease forever—

No amount of money, wealth, or reputation can redeem a soul. Scripture says to stop it forever. Only One can redeem the soul. Why waste time with any other method? Hear my words. Listen to my plea. Cut it out.

Wealth did not bring the soul, of Adam, into being. Love brought Adam into being. The Spirit of Love in the image of Christ ransomed salvation for every soul under heaven. This passage of scripture goes on to describe the place where unredeemed souls will reside. The very place that Christ entered to obtain the keys of death, hell, and the grave. Christ's finished work of the cross is the only ransom for a soul.

Therefore, stop trying to earn what is priceless. The value of which cannot be measured in earthly accounting. A debt so costly God had to send Himself to satisfy the price.

Psalm 33:19

To deliver their soul from death,

And to keep them alive in famine.

This is part of the wonderworking power discussed earlier. This faith not only delivers the soul from death but also keeps us alive in famine. A famine occurs when there is not enough sustenance to survive. Food and water sustain the body, while the Word of God sustains the spirit of a human.

Look at the power of this faith. It provides for the soul, which is not seen by the naked eye, as well as for the physical being. He provides what the pride of life cannot. He offers what lust fails to deliver. He is attentive to those who hope in Him. These facts remind me of the feeding of the multitudes. Christ delivered the Word of God to feed the spirit of the people and also provided food for them to eat until they were satisfied.

The multitudes hungered and thirsted for something to satisfy their souls. The provision of the Pharisees did not accomplish this. In all honesty, the Pharisees were taking from the multitudes to fill their own lusts and pride.

Christ, in contrast, was a loving and caring God watching over His creation, knowing all things that pertain to them. He lovingly, compassionately, and earnestly doted on Adam. Even after Adam's disobedience, His concern was for Adam's well-being.

There were consequences for the disobedience. However, those consequences stemmed from Perfect Love, unhindered Love, not wrath.

Proverbs 11:30

The fruit of the righteous is a tree of life,

And he who wins souls is wise.

A Tree of Life. Ironic words here, since the tree God suggested Adam eat from was the Tree of Life. The goodness that God desires us to seek exists in the Tree of Life.

All that we need is provided for in the Tree of Life. The giving of Life lies in the Spirit of God who leads us and guides us into all Truth. The Spirit of Life leads us and guides us into all Truth.

The second part of this scripture says that he who is wise wins souls. Victory. The win comes when one entreats a soul to choose to eat from the Tree of Life.

The beginning of wisdom is to revere God. Isn't that the same lesson Adam would have done well to heed? Over the course of all time the choice has been simple: choose to eat from the Tree of Life to give Life to your soul.

Section II: The Building is Specific

Luke 12:19

And I will say to my soul, "Soul, you have many goods laid up for many years; take your ease; eat, drink, and be merry."

This passage of scripture seems like a blessing if it stands alone. Actually, it is part of a parable about a rich fool. The line is what the rich fool says about his possessions. No better picture of one feeding his soul the fruit of the lust of the eyes, the pride of life, and the lust of the flesh. As I have been examining in the first part of this constructional, the soul is the product of the mind's choices. Here, the rich young fool is fat and happy without regard to a relationship with God.

"Take joy," he says to his soul, "in all that you have created. You are your own God, in other words. You must bow down to no one. There is nothing worth having that you cannot get for yourself." This folly is the same logic that created the downfall of man, the first soul. "Why are you concerned about what God said? You have the power to choose for yourself and take control of your own soul right here, right now. What can it really hurt?" All of Satan's arguments to the woman because she was misinformed or uninformed about the true nature of God.

How often are present-day souls bamboozled because of lack of understanding of the true nature of God? Laziness and lack of conviction allow many to be led astray. And leave the wellness of their souls to someone who seeks to destroy it and not build it up. What will you choose to say to your soul?

Matthew 22:37

Jesus said to him, "'You shall love the Lord your God with all your heart, with all your soul, and with all your mind.'

Perhaps you will choose to answer as the scripture says above. This is the answer Christ gives when asked about the greatest commandment. It's the perpetual theme in scripture, wouldn't you say? If we choose, within the authority of our free will, wouldn't our lives be peaceable? At least internally, wouldn't we choose for our lives to be peaceable? With eternal peace and the power of God, one can speak to the external and have them do as the soul wishes. A soul that loves the LORD, God with all, can change the atmosphere around them.

Isn't that just what the second man (I Corinthians 15:45) did? The second Adam changed the atmosphere and overcame obstacles wherever He went. He even told the wind and the waves to cease. Are all of these not promises Christ made to His disciples? And even a promise to do greater works than Him, John 14:12.

Those without wisdom believe that these greater works can be attained without taking stock of the soul. (If it can, I would have to ask from what spirit the works are being generated.) If any vessel is not completely used for one purpose over another, then what is the impact on the atmosphere? If one can be tossed to and fro by every wind of doctrine, what good is that being for the Kingdom of God (Ephesians 4:14)?

A soul that is set on pleasing the lusts and pride of this world cannot be wholly trusted to establish the Kingdom of God. Notice I did not say a person who is not perfect. I said a soul not set on loving God with ALL.

Psalm 6:3

My soul also is greatly troubled;
But You, O Lord—how long?

A perfect example of a soul set wholly on loving God. Even when it is in dismay, it cries out to God. What better example of a flawed man but a perfect witness before God?

No matter the skirmishes David encountered, even ones of his own making, he always returned to his God. After getting caught up with the things of this life, he faithfully returned to the LORD of his soul for counsel.

In the depths of his soul, David knew in Whom he believed. There was no other that could satisfy. The appointment on David's life was great, therefore so were his challenges. When ordinary men and women are designed as vessels of honor, the enemy of those souls works harder to structure their demise. The glory of the appointment is not for the individual man or woman but for God, which is why the enemy hates it.

The frailty of the human frame is usually not well hidden from one who seeks to destroy the vessel. Therefore, if one speaks to and builds up the soul before the appointment, the better off one will be under the pressure.

David had trained physically and, dare I say, mentally and even to a certain extent spiritually before his appointment as King. However, his soul was still battling with the issues of life. Perhaps his soul still harbored the treatment of his earthly father, the abandonment of his mother, the ridicule of his brothers, and the all-so-present rejection of all of them. The effects of these came to bear, although he was a mighty man of valor. The uncleansed soul had something to prove.

The proving came about by acquiring another man's wife. (Multiple times, I might add.) And the steps taken to cover up his corrupt actions with Bathsheba prove that he was a vessel that was not complete and content in the knowledge of his Creator. Yet after all the trials, David cried out to the LORD in dismay.

Psalm 84:2

My soul longs, yes, even faints
For the courts of the Lord;
My heart and my flesh cry out for the living God.

One thing I've learned is that when a soul has dwelled in the courts of the LORD, there is no substitute for the time spent in this place. Experiencing the presence of God is indescribable and incomparable. I am forever changed because of the presence of God tangibly in my life.

"My heart and flesh sing for joy for the living God." This fact is what has allowed me to live for God and not my flesh. There were breaches in my soul that occurred in my childhood that manifested in carnal ways when I became an adult. However, once the Spirit of the LORD began to draw me closer to the Lover of my soul, it became tantamount to my allegiance to my LORD.

I stopped making decisions based solely on my flesh because it was acceptable and even expected from a world that encouraged fulfillment of the lust of the flesh. It was no longer an option for me, though. Because my soul had visited the courts of the LORD, my flesh no longer controlled my actions.

Nothing on earth is like being in complete fellowship with the living God. Until one experiences it on their own, there is no alternative that can be shared to make someone believe how amazing it is to be in the courts of God. The flesh cannot receive such divine revelation.

Another point is this type of joy cannot be faked. Either one has it, or one does not. This is a longing and yearning that is palpable. Those who know that longing and yearning can identify it in others. It is hard not to be offended when someone deceitfully attempts to appropriate such intimacy. However, because of the presence of God, the one who has genuinely experienced this level of intimacy only wants others to truly experience it.

Psalm 142: 7

Bring my soul out of prison,
That I may praise Your name;
The righteous shall surround me,
For You shall deal bountifully with me."

Praise God. This is exactly what the LORD did for me. That is the reason my hands go up in praise, the reason I can dance without a care for who's watching.

If anything, what I would really like to know is why some can watch me and not praise the LORD for themselves. Still prisoners. Prisoners to the draw of this world. Prisoners to comparing what one has over another. Prisoners to the shallowness of a life of appeasing the flesh.

I recall the days of being a prisoner. Living for the approval of the creation as opposed to the Creator. So shackled and bound that I couldn't lift my voice or my hands because I was trying to fit into a religious mold.

Not so anymore. I am seeing myself surrounded by the righteousness of God. Surprise, it is not necessarily in the church building. The house of God is intended to be the atmosphere where souls are set free. Unfortunately, that is not always the case. It is often the place where souls are most bound yet have learned to put on the act that is acceptable in most places.

Ritual has become the largest prison of all. It takes no thought of the condition of the soul to follow a rite. A rite can be followed by the flesh and no one is the wiser. Literally. Yet ritual cannot ever deliver the bound. Only the Spirit of the Living God can do that.

Psalm 116:7

Return to your rest, O my soul,
For the Lord has dealt bountifully with you.

There are times when I do not feel at ease. I have termed it "being out of sorts." These time periods are not easy to describe, but I know when I am in them.

And I have to do exactly what this psalm says: remind myself of what God has done in my life. I recall the place I was in before the LORD drew me close. I recall the consequences of my actions and realize where I could be. Soon the rest and peace of my soul returned.

The rest that my soul seeks is in the presence of God. When worship is the place that I dwell. When seeking the peace of God in the midst of internal and external chaos is my aim. I understand the bounty that the LORD has afforded me. A priceless bounty that came at the price of Christ's deity.

What reason do I have to be ill at ease? All things are held together by Him (Colossians 1:17). Therefore, if I am in Christ, I should never be "out of sorts."

Psalm 121:7

The Lord shall [a]preserve you from all evil;
He shall preserve your soul.

Is there significance in the fact that the soul is the focus? Why didn't the Psalm say He will protect your flesh? Matthew 10:28 says, "Don't be afraid of those who want to kill your body; they cannot touch your soul. Fear only God, who can destroy both soul and body in hell."

This tells us a great deal. The power of God to redeem our souls, of course. However, the fact that there is none outside the body that can touch our soul. The only two beings that have authority when it comes to our soul are God and ourselves. We must control our souls by the authority of God. The soul is the eternal part of our existence. The spirit of a man will return to God, but the soul can be destroyed in hell with the body by the authority of the Most High God.

The Holy Spirit leads us into all Truth which engages our intellect. So, with knowledge, we speak the Truth of God to our souls. The mind must instruct the soul, which I discussed in the first part of this constructional.

We can rest in the knowledge that the Creator of the universe keeps our souls. When Adam ate from the wrong tree, his flesh

39

lost the ability to live forever, not the soul. Adam's and Eve's bodies were put out of the Garden, yet they and their descendants still maintained fellowship with God. It was in a different manner than when they existed in the Garden of Eden though.

Psalm 62:5

My soul, wait silently for God alone,
For my [a]expectation is from Him.

The writer of the psalm, David, admonishes his own soul to depend only on God. He acknowledges that you cannot put your trust in victory in anyone or anything else.

Furthermore, he instructs the reader and the hearer of the psalm in the same way. Victory comes only from the LORD. So why would you put your hope in idols such as riches, power, intellect, yourself, or others? Hope can only rest on the LORD, your God.

Again, we find David speaking direct authority to his soul. Soul, do as you are told. According to what David has encountered with God, he gives instruction to his innermost being.

The soul obeys. The question is, what are we telling it to obey? We can only instruct our souls according to our understanding and knowledge. Therefore, if we are not following the leading of the Holy Spirit into all Truth, then our souls are being led astray by misinformation and ignorance.

If you are attempting to reach a physical destination with faulty instructions, will you ever make it to the destination? The same holds true for our souls. Are we leading our souls to righteousness or destruction?

Proverbs 13:19

A desire accomplished is sweet to the soul,
But it is an abomination for fools to depart from evil.

Praise God! An excellent next step to the previous construct. Desire realized is sweet to the soul. The second part of the proverb emphasizes that the desires of our souls should be godly.

I was just summing up the fact that the authority we take over our souls should be driven by the desire for Truth from the Holy Spirit. To turn away from evil is, in essence, to repent.

The desire we realize after we repent from evil is the destiny and purpose God designed for us before the foundation of the earth. God the Father gave us the second Adam, a life-giving spirit, as a conduit for our repentance to resolve the transgression of the first Adam, the soul.

Therefore, we must turn away from our wicked ways and choose life. The Adam and Eve opportunity all over again; turn away from the tree of the knowledge of good and evil and choose the Tree of (eternal) Life.

Proverbs 16:24

Pleasant words are like a honeycomb,
Sweetness to the soul and health to the bones.

Here's the thing: pleasant words can only come from a soul that has been transformed. Have you ever met someone who cannot say "I love you"? I mean honestly and truthfully cannot get the words to come out of their mouth? As if the words are arrested before entering the atmosphere.

Of course, before I started taking the initiative and time to care for my own soul, I would take a lack of "I love you" personally. Because you know what, at one point, I could not say it either. Growing up in a household that did not know the true meaning of hope. A household that, unfortunately, believed that the answer to life's ills was the very thing I have discussed that corrupts one's soul.

The lust of the flesh and eye, along with the pride of life, creates a void that can never be filled. When one lives their life from a void, trying to fill the void with things empty of value, then misery is multiplied.

The proverb states healing to the bones. Healing with words brings to mind the scripture that says, "Out of the abundance of the heart, the mouth speaks." What is the heart but the manifestation of the soul? If the soul is not well and attended to, then the fountains from the heart will be polluted.

The last thing this world needs is more pollution. The very earth is groaning for the sweetness and healing that comes from the sons of God. The outcomes of our communities depend on the souls of those who make up the communities.

Proverbs 25:25

As cold water to a weary soul,
So is good news from a far country.

Only when I began to fast from all beverages except water did I fully appreciate its goodness? Someone said that the more water you drink, the more you want nothing but water. I have found that to be true.

If one never had water or had so little of it that they preferred another beverage, then the value of water would be lost on them. Until they are so parched that their body is screaming out for the substance that replenishes their life source.

As I was just speaking of a polluted soul, so has become our desire for purity. We have become a population that has become accustomed to bad news from distant lands: famine, strife, murder, war, pestilence, and so on, that good news is not given its proper value.

What would happen if we fasted from bad news? Only let good news into our psyche? Would we begin to crave it so much so that we actually began to instigate it?

And I mean the true good news. The purity of the gospel: "that God so loved the world He sent His only begotten Son so that any who believes on Him would have life and that more abundantly." The good news that actually fills the void. Not the things that the adversary has been trying to sell since Adam was in the Garden.

Adam was in the place where God dwelt, yet he was swayed by the promise of the report of the knowledge of good and evil instead of pledging his allegiance to the tree that brought on the abundance of Good News. Adam, the soul, was swayed.

Proverbs 2:10

When wisdom enters your heart,
And knowledge is pleasant to your soul,

Another scripture states that the fear of God is the beginning of wisdom. So, in essence, Proverbs 2:10 states, "The fear of God will enter your heart and the knowledge will be pleasant to your soul." Have you noticed that the further society gets away from the reverence (fearing) of God, the more society is obstinate to real knowledge?

Opinions and experts are prevalent on every major television station. However, aren't the reporters using their own basis of knowledge, not one based on any solid foundation? Even worse still is the fact that the news being reported is nothing short of propaganda from the richest, most popular, and most beautiful people.

The days of experiencing a profound conversation based on facts and analytical thought are gone. The monster that has taken its place is vapid and empty. Dare I say resembling nothing but the lust of the flesh, the lust of the eyes, and the pride of life.

For example, unconscious bias is being used synonymously with racism. Racism is an outward expression whereas unconscious bias is an inward reality which is the condition of one's soul. I agree that unconscious bias can manifest as racism. Yet racism is only one of the manifestations that can arise from unconscious bias.

Deuteronomy 13:3

you shall not listen to the words of that prophet or that dreamer of dreams, for the Lord your God is testing you to know whether you love the Lord your God with all your heart and with all your soul

God Himself dictated the order of this construction. He was building something with me to share with you all. This construction would be useless if it did not construct Tara first. During my walk with God, I have been given some awesome words about my future. Also, I have experienced some incredibly unbelievable events. Yet, through it all, I made a decision to focus on what my LORD would have me do.

If I were to have chosen by the lust of the flesh, lust of the eyes, and the pride of life, my end would have been vastly different. I have never been one to take the easy or well-worn route. I want the route that is created just for me. Because of this, I have trouble understanding why anyone would want to claim someone else's path as their own.

Our Father in Heaven is so in love with each one of His creation that He wrote a uniquely individual script for each of us. Each script was written perfectly for our character type, body type, voice registry, and all the other things that make us unique.

Therefore, this scripture simply says, after all is said and done in this life, will you choose Me? A basic yet profound question. It is the same question God has been asking the soul since He created it. The age-old question each soul has to answer before entering eternity.

All the other is just frills and fancy. The scriptures are a means to satisfy a rational mind. A loving Father presenting every opportunity for His creation to willingly choose Him. So, in this constructional, when you get right down to the nitty-gritty, after getting to the heart and soul of the matter: the Father, Son, and Holy Spirit is asking, do you choose Me?

Section III: The Upkeep is Personal

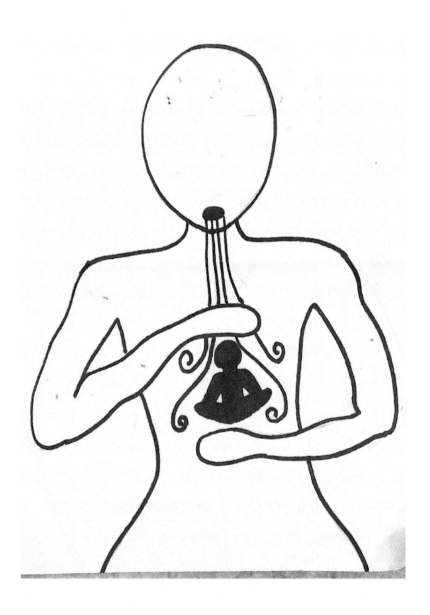

The same as any makeover you want to maintain, you must put in the work daily. Once the makeover is complete, the work and activities that went into the makeover are followed to maintain the new state of being. Any permanent change requires repetitive actions to continue the manifestation. When beginning a new makeup regiment, the different applications now needed compared to your old regiment must be done continually in order for it to become the new way of living.

I do know a few things about makeup and do not consider it a sin against God. However, the issue I have with it is when it is used to present a façade of wholeness when the vessel itself is crumbling. The best example I can give in the form of a personal story is when I got out of the hospital after being brought back to the land of the living. I went to a popular cosmetic retail store to purchase makeup. I wasn't planning to buy a lot, just something to improve what I thought was a deficiency in my appearance. I asked the salesperson what she would recommend. She said, "You don't need any makeup". Wait. What! Her job was to sell, and she told me I didn't need makeup.

Perhaps I should mention that as soon as I woke up in the hospital and was taken off the ventilator, I asked for my Bible. And my TV stayed on the local channel that preached the Gospel. Now, I did not have a deathbed conversion, and I was doing these activities daily before my physical death experience.

This is the reason it bothers me tremendously when there are carriers of the Gospel who are commanding that followers of God do the things that the world does to appear whole. I must ask them if their fruit has insecticides and artificial preservatives in order to look like the fruits of the Spirit.

Daily Maintenance

Foundations and upkeep occur in another industry, construction. Carpenters, electricians, plumbers, and other skilled tradesmen learn the basics of building. Although every house that they work on will not look the same, there are principles and skills that can be used in every home in terms of basic maintenance. The pipes may be copper or polyvinyl chloride. The wood may be oak instead of pine. The current may be AC instead of DC. However, a skilled workman knows how to address the differences.

The same is true for each one of us. The Master Builder used the same basic blueprint for mankind. Eyes, ears, feet, emotions, reasoning, and so on. However, each individual has a different maintenance requirement and schedule. Anyone can read the other chapters and follow the same basic principle to get the results I anticipate.

Yet, the daily approach will definitely be different. And will probably change throughout their lifetime. When I graduated from college and began my first professional job, I used the Franklin Covey planner. Now, everyone is not going to use this planner for whatever reason. Truthfully, some of the people I have met have a picture of me burning in hell for referencing anything to do with Benjamin Franklin because of what history tells us about his beliefs and practices.

But scripture tells me that "we know that God causes everything to work together for the good of those who love God and are called according to His purpose for them" Romans 8:28. So if my eyes are on my LORD and Savior as I walk along the path that He has selected for me before the foundation of the earth then Ben Franklin's method can only mean good to me.

I am a proponent of doing exactly what God is leading an individual to do. Many would warn that you should only do what is in the scriptures and will hold up a Bible and wave it at you as an illustration. But it is also written in scripture that "...there are also many other things that Jesus did, which if they were written one by one, I suppose that even the world itself could not contain the books that would be written. Amen" John 21:25

Also, John the Disciple tells us that Christ said, "Most assuredly, I say to you, he who believes in Me, the works that I do he will also do; and greater works than these he will do, because I go to My Father." John 14:12. God Himself bids us to do great exploits in His name. So why would we shrink back from the power and authority that His sacrifice and return to the throne at the right hand of the Father affords us?

Anyone who expects you to shrink back or not live up to the full potential of God's Grace and blessing upon your life does not know Him intimately. Those who live for Him and are in Him and He in them live to bring Glory to the Father by honoring the Son. Those constrictions created by man are only to stifle the good works that God has set forth for His creation to accomplish. Human beings are afraid of letting the worship of God loose because then they will not be able to control it.

In the Old Testament Moses was sent to liberate God's people in order for them to worship Him. The Israelites were in constant drudgery from sunrise to sunset and only had the drive to eat, sleep and repeat the same drudgery. Isn't that the same as the American worker is operating today?

American children are taught that the American Dream is to work 5 days a week, at least 40 hours a week, in an office that you spend 30 minutes or more to get to every morning to receive pay to give to the masters of rent (or mortgage), electricity, food salesman, taxes, and any other salesman you are privileged to afford with the pay you receive for expending at minimum one-fourth of your life every week. Consider another fourth of your life during the week, if you are blessed, is spent resting from the mental and physical exhaustion that the fourth spent at work demands.

Now, if you are blessed to have a family: spouse, children, parents, siblings, then you try to squeeze out the percentage of time for fellowship with them. However, if one is to chase that American Dream, then this is the portion that gets appropriated somewhere at the bottom of the list. Regulated to those holidays that have been approved by the Pharaohs. Again, no rest is afforded to those who are preparing for the celebration or gathering. So, the respite turns into another opportunity to serve the masters, much like the Israelites, who God sent Moses to liberate so they could worship Him.

Why do we let outside forces dictate our comings and goings? Is it good old-fashioned programming? If nothing else, technology has taught us that programming can change to suit different circumstances and to render different results. Before getting the Franklin Covey planner I was not programmed to believe that the little successes everyday would have an outcome on my larger successes way down the road.

The planner had me prioritize my now in line with the future I wanted to accomplish. And it didn't just include the tasks that were necessary to maintain that 9 to 5 to get to the perceived American Dream. The planner took me through exercises that challenged me to determine what was important to me. Where did I want to be in 5, 10, or 20 years? What type of person did I want to be as I traveled along the way? What kind of relationship did I desire with the list of people I put down as important?

Since I professed Christ the year I graduated from college, the first who that I put down was a child of God. I wanted to embrace all that meant. It didn't happen overnight but as I put in that planner everyday something to get me closer to God it worked.

It worked so that the foundation that I built with the planner became my way of life. I was walking out what the planner had trained me to do with all of the exercises to teach me self-awareness. Which, when you think about it, is what the scriptures are designed to do. I was not raised going to the church building every Sunday. My foundation of the scriptures started when I was about to turn 30. I began going to church that went through the scriptures verse by verse and taught about the history surrounding the text. Once again, setting a foundation that I would use as I grew more intimate with the author of the scriptures and the author of my faith. The foundation that keeps me ever present with my LORD. The foundation that spurs me to seek the life God created for me before the foundation of the earth.

If I would have depended on someone else's revelation of the life God has for me, it may not be true to the author because of their thoughts and feelings about me. Me as a person. Me as a woman. Me as a child of my parents. More importantly, the revelation that they received about my life may have nothing at all to do with me but with them and their outlook on life. Therefore, I would be held hostage to another Pharaoh trying to get their dream accomplished from the sweat of my brow such that the dream that God created expressly for me would never get accomplished.

Many who walk in church circles have this doctrine of covering. You have to have a covering from a man or woman who apparently has been in ministry longer than you. Some have even made it akin to the covering that Jewish men wear in the temple. Everyone can wear the same covering and all those who have chosen a man or woman as their covering can even have the same person covering them. But does that mean that the covering is operating the same for each of those individuals?

For example, if a man covers someone who has seen angelic beings and he has not, what is he covering. In this example, it would appear to me that the one who has not had experiences with angelic beings would be covering the person who has with unbelief or, even worse, doubt. The covering could be keeping someone from the greater works that God has promised those who believe simply by not believing. So why would anyone want to be covered by that?

It's not bragging or boasting except for in Christ, who gave His life for those who believe Him to operate in the greater. Not to have a form of godliness but to deny the power.

Since beginning this construction, I have started a ROKU Channel: gloWhole Inward Repair Outward Result. The vision was to document others' stories about overcoming. Scripture tells us in Revelation that "they overcame by the Blood of the Lamb and the word of their testimony." I've learned while walking that it takes a certain strength to share your testimony. Especially if it is more than "the LORD got me the car of my dreams or the house of my dreams". Which actually isn't the testimony. The testimony is the part that happened that did not look all that glamorous. The part that proves our Father in Heaven was present through the entire circumstance, not only at the dealership or the lawyer's office where the mortgage documentation was signed.

Our Father promised to never leave us or forsake us. This book is the evidence of that fact. I started this book several years ago. During that time, I was unemployed for a short period after working in a highly toxic environment. During that period of time, I attempted to help someone else write a book.

Please note that I put as much effort into projects that I have committed to as I do my own projects. So, when the person I was assisting no longer had interest in the project, I had to choose how I would respond. Thank God I was in the middle of researching scriptures about the soul. Honestly, giving credit where it is due, it was this person who prompted me to start studying about the soul. I presume that goes back to the Scripture I mentioned earlier about all things working for good.

By getting more knowledge and understanding about the soul, I was able to use wisdom in my actions and emotions. I began to understand that even if I was handed disrespect and lack of compassion by someone else, I did not have to take the bait. That is growth because I was a firm believer in a holy hissy fit. My definition of a holy hissy fit is when you make your point about the injustice handed to you as logically as possible but perhaps not at a modulated level. Also, since I am a writer, I have perfected the non-verbal holy hissy fit as well.

Now, I began to truly understand that walking with God means He is your constant companion. Yes, as children of our Father in Heaven, we will face trials and tribulations. Some were invited because of the choices we made, and others were imposed upon us. Yet God delivers us from them all.

Recently, I was speaking with a coach assigned to me through a "higher learning" platform. (I'll explain the quotations a little later.). They asked me why I didn't share the harder parts of my story. Why only the parts that teach a lesson? And they insinuated that there was something not normal about it. As I began to unpack the question, it made me realize that they were operating under the assumption that I owed them every part of my story. The fact of the matter is that I don't owe a person anything but to love them. We got to the question because I gave two examples of people studying me intensely to find my flaws. Somehow, the person attributed the behavior of the people I described as my failure for not allowing my flaws to hang out.

I cannot be 100% certain but I do not believe this person follows Christ or is a fan of anyone who does. Therefore, I find it equally troubling that this person would dare to know me after speaking with me for a total of no more than 2 hours over 3 months.

Again, I was afforded the opportunity to choose how to respond. Interestingly enough, this person is a growth coach. They offered me all the trite activities I should use to become self-aware. Even though they had complimented me for being self-aware earlier in the session, I could have responded by saying that I had already made those activities a part of my path beginning in high school when my advanced English teacher suggested them. I could have directed them to my online blog, which I kept for nearly 4 years, where I discussed my struggles and my growth publicly. Or perhaps just provide her with a rough draft of this book.

However, I did none of those things. I just clarified the assignment and bid farewell until the next session. This brings me back to the main topic of the constructional. The soul. If we do not allow our Father in Heaven access to cleanse, repair, and renew our souls then someone else will assume responsibility and build our soul for us.

I'll end this in the same way I began. Others vehemently disagree and lash out when I reference the Scripture about being made perfect as the Father and Son are perfect. The Godhead provides a third Person to lead and guide us into all Truth, perfection if you will. It makes me consider that anyone who does not want you to walk according to the leading and guiding of our Father in Heaven would like you to mold yourself into an image they deem acceptable and not the image of God.

Now, I can discuss the "higher learning" that I placed in quotation marks earlier. During the time that I have been writing this book I have sought knowledge about the origins of man and Scriptures. When studying Scripture the vastness and intricacies could overwhelm us. In all of my getting I sought to get understanding to the point that I can explain what I have learned.

I learned that our "higher education" institutions were created with the agenda to impede as much creative thought as possible. The "higher learning" is to manufacture automatons unless you are found to have a skill or gift that can be manipulated for the sole purpose of making the wealthy even wealthier. So, at best, one can become a cash cow for someone who is higher in social and/or economic stature. Do not be deceived. This does not only occur in worldly environments. Unfortunately, there are also holy cash cows. So, one is either a cash cow or a watched rebel who attempts to operate outside of the status quo.

By taking a look at history, we can witness the manipulation of facts and accounts since before man was created. An entity has counterfeited the story of the Father's Creation with several false narratives to deceive many. Yet, instead of allowing the Father's children to establish their own relationship with the Father, some have tried to control the body of Christ to the point of dictatorship. Teaching that some know more than the other children and should not be questioned.

When the children know the Father for themselves the personal revelation allows the child to optimize the gifts the Father gave them specifically. This keeps the brethren from having to sift through a message made for a thousand or more once or twice a week. The answers from God would be individual, so that each individual can build the Kingdom, because our Father in Heaven has constructed them.

Sadly, the world is trying to turn compassion, empathy, and the other characteristics of the Son into unnatural robots. No matter the tweaks and behavior modifications, human frailty cannot score 100% across a board of unrealistic metrics. However, by following Christ, being led by the Holy Spirit, and basking in the Love of the Father, one can become more and more like their perfect Creator. The one whose image of man and woman was created.

SATISFY

You are beautiful, You make even the simple things works of art

All of Your creation is astonishing to behold. So many perfect examples of Your handiwork I don't know where to start.

As You draw me closer to You I realize the world as You intended it for man

The beauty of the ocean, the power of the sea, the vastness of the sky, all of Your majesty, in awe I stand.

All Your creation You made for the enjoyment of Your image, Your likeness that You made from dust.

Yet we turned away from it for the pride of life, the lust of the eyes, and still You loved us.

You're awesome in power and awesome in love

You sent Your only Begotten to save us; He is the glory from above

My heart has such a yearning to be with You; closer than any two souls on earth can connect.

The searching I've been doing in the world only leaves my heart with sorrowful regret.

The ache l have to be enveloped by Your perfect love is only aned by the presence of Your Spirit and Your Word. ng to remedy that ache with the devices of man is absurd.

Everything I've done that draws me away.from You were done to please I

Now, I know the things of God are the only things that truly satisfy.

Use Me

My soul is restless; without calm

I know there is something I need to do for the Kingdom at this very hour

As David wrote in the one hundred and tenth Psalm

"Thy people (shall be) willing in the day of thy power"

I'm willing Lord, full of zeal, courage, and drive Although current circumstances have me stalled in park

Sharing Your Gospel, singing Your praises, devouring Your Word is all I need to feel alive

Each day I get to know You the fire in my soul ignites with the tiniest Godly spark

I long to commune with You; which in and of itself presents an inconsistence

Because only in You is my hope ever to be accomplished

God You are my divine inspiration

My sole supplier of salvation

Each morning, noon, and night it is Your complete justice i desire
Unlike the common man I place all that is of me under subjection
to Your Holy Fire

Burn me up; blow me away; I beg of You from time to time I ask
You that not in jest; I'm serious because I want You to keep me
focused as I continue to climb

Let not my purpose sway; serving You is my ultimate reward
Finally, I've got it untwisted; honoring You is why I press forward

Forward and through

I'ma keep pressin' until I'm face to face with You

UNENDING

Someone loves me genuinely, purely

My experience with past love has left me jaded to all who attempt to demonstrate this feeling

Even what I once thought was a feeling I realized was a choice One decides to love another; it's not the accelerated beating of the heart or the queasy uneasiness that establishes a love that is true

It's the unwavering decision to commit to, support, encourage, strengthen, protect, adore. The list is infinite; I can't believe I have all those and more. And because I have them I must decide to impart the same. Because I am loved thusly the decision is quite easy.

The way God intended. He intends for us to give love purely. The way He gave it to us in the pure sacrifice of His only begotten Son.

He chose to offer His Son as redemption for a lost people.

Jesus Christ chose His church and He committed to it, strengthens it, protects it, adores it, the list is infinite.

So husbands love your wives the same so that they will impart same to your children, your family, your friends, you and a dying world

The cycle started so long ago with that Babe in a manger. Now you must choose to impart the same because you are loved in such a fashion.

PURE HEART

His ways are not our ways

And for that we should be thankful

His power and mercy endure forever

But our courage and compassion can end in a day

His joy can make us leap, scream, shout, and cry all in the same breath

We allow our sorrow to still all that He has promised us

Let go of the very thing that holds you from Him Because that is the only way you can be free

It's also the only way you can see what He has in store for you

The grip you have on the things of the world causes the things of God to slip through your fingers

If you are constantly focused on Him you wouldn't have the energy to cause vindication you think you are justified by the means of your own standards

A pure heart does not hold a grudge or look for wrongdoing

It doesn't spend its time focused on backstabbing or double-dealing

A pure heart is more concerned with the things

God would have it pursuing

Not concentrating on the best way to hurt someone's feelings

A pure heart loves all those that need love

It doesn't pick and choose based on criteria only man understands

A pure heart wraps itself around the tasks that were instructed from above

The motives of this heart is evidenced by the work of the hands

FOUNDATION TO FINISHING

A pure heart offers service to all mankind

Not just to those that generate monetary wealth

A pure heart is most difficult to find

Once your life has been impacted by one so rare you will see a significant improvement in your emotional health

LET ME INTRODUCE YOU

I maybe strange to you

You don't know who I am

This you should know I'm only a visitor to this land.

Not put here to stay

My life here is only temporary

Commissioned to pay my dues on earth to guarantee my existence
for all eternity.

Living to honor God, the Trinity

Following the course He has laid out just for me

There is no competition for those who live for Christ.

Because if your earthly father desires to give each of his children
good gifts

How much more would your Father in heaven desire to provide for
you

FOUNDATION TO FINISHING

Just look at the example of the sacrifice of his only begotten Son;
that demonstrates love that is unselfishly true.

He is waiting for you to ask and lay down your life for His way

For all He has already generously given that is a minuscule price
to pay

He wants to be in close fellowship with you

So close that all your trials, heartache, and pain don't touch you
but rests on His shoulders.

Come near me, He calls. Praise my name on high.

Wrap yourself in His joyous light id your soul will never die.

Honor Him, Praise Him, Worship Him submit all your love to Him
solely.

For all the things of this earth will pass away. But God and all His
things will remain familiar on this earth and beyond. With His
love you are assured of a brighter day.

SEARCHING TO FIND

Peace on earth, Peace be unto you May they rest in peace, Peace of mind

All are searching but peace is so elusive, hard to find

What are you employing to find it?

How will you know when it's yours; will your seeking quit?

It appears you're working mighty hard to capture something that

should make you serene.

It can't be that hard to find; it's not like it's something no one has

ever seen.

Or has it been seen? Did you check the lost and found?

What good is your searching when I see your hands are bound.

FOUNDATION TO FINISHING

I'm sorry...l'm mistaken, you're fully incarcerated.

Locked up, held up, fed up, caught up, not a thing to be celebrated.

No, I'm wrong again you deserve an award; a Pulitzer Prize.

For carrying a burden of that magnitude and size.

Maybe that's what you're looking for, "All glory to you."

You don't need what's good, pure, everlasting, and true.

If you did, you'd realize it's not elusive; hard to find.

All you do is call on the name of Jesus when you realize you're in a bind.

What's more; if continual praise is on your lips.

You'll find that peace is never outside of your grips.

His name is Jesus, yes, also known as the Prince of Peace.

Worship and Praise Him and you'll find your release.\

FEED MY SOUL LORD

Lord, I long for intimate time with You

To feast on Your perfect pleasures and delicacies

My soul needs nourishment only You can provide through Your Spirit

I've felt famished lately, as if I'm missing my important, essential nutrients

I'm depleted Lord, I want to be filled with You More and more of You

Without Your strengthening sustenance

I have no energy to do Your work

Feed my soul Lord I'm famished

The meat of Your Word is what I long to savor

FOUNDATION TO FINISHING

Feed me, Lord I am starving

A diet filled with too much of the world leaves me sluggish and malnourished

Feed me Lord with Your satisfying fare

The food of the world must be pleasing to the eye to be appetizing

But Your delectables are pleasing to the Spirit. A soul can't wait to gorge on Your goodness.

Perfect sweetness, absolutely fulfilling

The more You feed me the more I can hold. Let me never get enough.

The craving I have is not quenched by any means save Your tender mercies and sustaining grace.

EYES DECEIVE

What do you see when you're looking at me?

I know what l'd hope you'd see

I'd hope you'd see that the Living God is housed in me completely

If that's not what your eyes show you as the true picture;

that I'm free

I've got more work to do; praying, reading the Word,

and surrendering to the Almighty

Now, what do you see when you're looking at me?

Is it possible that you see me as my eyes see

I see someone whose held captive by God completely

Yet I don't feel caged; I'm totally free

I'm at liberty to do the will of the Almighty

Finally what do you see looking at me?

FOUNDATION TO FINISHING

I hope it's now visible for all the world to see

That I am enveloped by the light of heaven completely

It's as if I'm soaring high above the world at peace and free
Undeniably worship, study, and praise has brought me into the

presence of the Almighty

COME FOR ME COME FOR US

Lord I look around and all I see

Is making my heart heavy

My only consolation is that You said these things must occur

For Your returning to be sure

Jesus, please come for me. Your Spirit is here among Your church and still I want my Savior to come for me.

The work to be done seems unbearable at times All this violence, apathy, and appalling crimes Now I understand why my elders always say

"Things weren't like this in my day"

Jesus won't You come for me. The evil is progressing. Yes the Comforter is able. My King will You come for me?

Everyday brings a new worldly reality

FOUNDATION TO FINISHING

It's not the flesh and blood, I know, it's the principality The darkness is pervading in every spot

The bit of leaven in Your church is beginning to leaven the whole lot

Father will You send Your Son to come for us? The louder the cries of Your people for souls to repent...the stronger the force against us. Lord come for us.

Your Spirit is working to unite us all

Across geographic boundaries, cultural divides, the multitudes are heeding Your call Persecution is trying to match the pace

Which is serving to strengthen our faith as we run the race

Does that make it any sooner for You to come for us? This world is perishing Your children are thirsting and hungering for You.

Come for us.

We're foreigners; not assimilating to worldly affairs

We're awaiting the return of Him, whom we cast all our cares

With hearts of hope and anticipation etched on our faces

We're looking forward to dwelling in mansions in the heavenly places

God we can't wait for You to come for us. We live each day praying for Your return. Father we know you know when our Prince will come.

I BELONG TO HIM

Before I was free, God still had His hold on me.

Even then I was obedient and always went where I was sent.

In the barren wilderness where it was my family surely I did miss.

I did as I was told although this place in its indiscretions was bold.

He was there with me and held my hand as He revealed the things

He wanted me to see.

He strengthened me and empowered me to have courage and conviction over what others would have deemed the ultimate restriction.

"Hold fast to My truths", He encouraged me to do. And there's nothing you won't conquer and from this experience my wisdom grew.

For this place was barren not of lush green trees and flowers. It lacked Love and it's inhabitants practiced greed and sought earthly powers.

They were striving to control their own fate. And what they presumed was covered by compassion was most assuredly hate.

You see they were awesome pretenders with what appeared to be good intentions. For sure they know the road to Hell is paved with self-serving imaginative inventions.

When it was all over who knows if I made any difference. I just know it was the beginning of me using the things of God as my only reference.

I AM WHO I AM

I have got a story to tell,

It's not about fairy tale lands and things of my imagination

It's about the royal lineage of which I am a relation

Let's get something clear before I continue

I may talk a lot in the first person as I spin my tale to you But trust, I do know to whom all glory and honor is due

In the beginning of this present journey there was darkness For the world and for me

I began seeking the Lord and asked God to perfect my testimony

I'm not the type to pull you aside and give you all the gory details I'm a creative person by nature, so I give everything my own personal flair Whereas some may say it's flamboyance I say it shows how much I care

TARA T TATE

I can't just put out a plate and a napkin for my guest

They must feel special when I have accepted the charge to entertain The simple may suffice but I find it exhilarating to spruce up the plain

God created me uniquely because He loved me so much Everything about me was created by His glorious design

And when one comes against me with ill-intentions in their heart He lovingly warns

"Take heed. She's mine."

I can't boast about my talents and gifts

You see adept skill and cleverness in the things I've done

I tell you it's not because of me but because I've been chosen by the Holy One

So I implore you don't think I'm self-promoting when I use the word Know that I know that you know where the glory and honor should lie

I know I'm blessed only because I'm the apple of His eye

And that took no effort on my part

It was all the work of the Trinity In the present His Spirit beckons

In the past the Father was in control when His Son died for me

I am who I am by no will of my own

I am who I am for no other reason than this

God is a God who loves and forgives and has promised me an eternity of bliss

The beauty of this story I'm telling you is that it could have various endings

It could have a different beginning, yes, it's true Because in all places where there is "j" and "me".

God wants you to replace it with "you"!

CALL TO ARMS: EXERCISE THE AUTHORITY

Born free? Or were you in captivity?

Yes, captivity. You were a slave to sin.

When you were a babe, it was not your own, but it was definitely sin you were in.

Bound and shackled trying to be free.

Can I tell you? Just between you and me.

There is only one way out of that lonely, dark cell.

The added bonus is you will also not experience hell.

This message is not only for those who don't have a relationship with Christ.

But also for those who already have eternal life.

Are you living a life that is pleasing to the King?

FOUNDATION TO FINISHING

Do you have faith that He can conquer everything?

Not just a few things, He should be the ruler in all your circumstances.

With the state of the world today why would you take any chances?

Let God be God. Give it all over to Him.

When you leave your fate to your own devices your odds of survival are none, not slim.

He gave you freedom. You accepted, you said.

But why is it you're still seeking salvation through your works. Don't you know you're still dead?

He died to give you life and privileges of the Kingdom.

But His people exercising His power is seen seldom.

Those whom the Son set free is free indeed.

But so many of His people are walking around sorely in need.

In need...when He has given us His awesome promises.

His word makes this clear; what part did you miss?

Don't get so wrapped up in yourself, you must let go.

You don't want to hear your name following God saying woe.

Whenever God uses "woe" the immediate outcome is not good.

That means your actions weren't as they should.

Now, He must chasten you not because of hate.

He wants to pull you back in line before it's too late.

Christian, die to yourself and give it over to God please.

Your way will not give you comfort and set your mind at ease.

He has given you access to Him and He is all you need.

Exercise the power He gave you when His Son said, "It is finished" and you were freed.

THE END

Don't let the sweet face fool you

Because all at once the wrath of the Lamb could come out of the
blue

The meek and humble Christians you now know

Will be removed and in their place there will be those who have to
show

You what is coming in the Seven Sealed Judgments

If you know what they know you'll fall on your face and repent

But how can you know what they know

Because if you haven't heard

You must go to the Sacred Book and read the Holy Word

The Sacred Book? Yes. The Bible!

FOUNDATION TO FINISHING

For within it are all things that Christians are held accountable

No end of grade testing or teacher made exam

The tests come continually for you to strengthen your faith in I
Am

No pass or fall grade. How will you know if you've succeeded?

During the sorting process the wheat will be weeded

Away from the chaff.

You may think you're fooling everyone.

But in reality you're only tricking those who can not see...that the
Rock you're stumbling over weighs more than a ton.

The Rock of Ages, He whom the builders rejected.

He does not have to be elected.

He was chosen by One; the only one that matters.

Even though as a babe He was clothed in rags that were in tatters.

He is royalty. We're not fit for the King.

Nothing can compare. No, not anything.

To the love He has given us; so freely He laid.

For the gift He gave us no amount of money can be paid.

To compensate Him for the Breath of Life.

He will place in your soul.

He has been with us from before the beginning of time and with us still until the days of old.

CAUGHT OR CAUGHT UP

You, man, are trying to free me

Instead of allowing the Son of Man to set me free

You, man, tell me not to let my family dominate my life

Then in the next breath declare your expectations which if not
met will cause you and I strife

You, man, listen to what you say

Not just when you're preaching, but also to those requests you
expect others to obey

The Son of Man is the one I'm to emulate

And all He's requesting is for me to be Tara Teressa Tate

Follow me, He said. That's Jesus talking

Is He in your sight? If not, stop balking and start walking

Pay strict attention to Him and cease worrying about things that are none of your affair

Or else when He returns you will not be caught up but caught unaware

BATTLE READY

The war is on whether we want to acknowledge it

Some want to bury their heads in the sand and pretend the enemy
is not actively seeking souls

My friends that is dangerous in more ways than I care to share

Of whom shall you fear if the Lord is for you

The Lord IS for you

The question remains are you for the Lord

Perhaps that's the true war you are fighting after all

You can't battle the enemy for others souls because you have not
fully won your own (Yet)

You better take claim of the "More than a conqueror Spirit" and live in it

Exude all the power and authority that term possesses.

For you are His and all glory is Thine

HOW

Do you know what to call me?

Do you know how to get my attention?

Call me a friend of God, I will listen.

How can you make that claim so bold?

How can you be certain He will claim you as His friend?

He told me in His Word and also that He will be with me unto the end.

You mean unto the ends of the earth? The end of the Age?

You don't think that's a mighty long way, a mighty long time?

No, not for the Lord; therefore in His wings I intend to hide.

Is there room enough for you?

Is it vast enough for all to go who wish?

Surely, this is God who fed the multitudes with four loaves and two fish.

If you are so certain about the God of whom you speak?

If He is so awesome how can He allow millions to perish?

It is not His will for anyone to succumb to the devil's wiles; believe me every soul on earth He does cherish.

What is this you say?

What with all the power He has, He can save whoever He wants; all?

Definitely, but we have some responsibility to, we must honor His call.

Did I miss His call or was I asleep when it came?

Did He only try once when I wasn't ready to hear?

His call is so persistent and timely you couldn't have missed it, do not fear.

Can I approach Him? I want to be sure I'm saved.

Can I give my life to Him now? I don't want to wait.

Certainly, pray for Him to come into your heart and you will be a friend of God on this date.

AGAIN

As I seek You not only do I find You I find all I need for a rewarding life

As I meditate on the things above I experience none of the world's strife

As I praise You to see Your face

I enjoy the splendor of Your presence

As I explore Your Word to know Your Holy instruction

I gain knowledge of Him whom i reverence

As I worship You in Spirit and Truth

I am given peace that surpasses all understanding

As I hunger and thirst for Your precious Word

FOUNDATION TO FINISHING

I am filled to overflowing, because You put the desire in me to want Your righteousness

As I sit and wonder how You will make my tomorrow better than my yesterday

I am astounded as You show up and claim my heart all over again

CHORUS:

As You call me

As You draw me

I'm coming back to You

HAVE I

Told You I love You

Shown You I love You

Declared endlessly my love for You

Loved Your people

Served Your people

Fed Your people

Increased Your Kingdom

Prepared for Your Kingdom

Stored treasures in Your Kingdom

Read Your Word

Obeyed Your Word

Meditated on Your Word

Thanked You for Your Son

Prayed to You through Your Son

Blessed You and Your Son

Clung to precepts that are holy

Kept my actions holy

Trained my mind to embrace thoughts that are holy

YOU HAVE

Told me You love me

Shown Your love for me

Declared endlessly Your love for me

Loved Your people

Served Your people

Fed Your people

Increased Your Kingdom

Prepared Your Kingdom

Stored my treasures in Your Kingdom

FOUNDATION TO FINISHING

Created me to obey Your Word

Provided peace for me to meditate on Your Word

Offered graciously for our sin Your Son

Set the advocate to You through Your Son

Blessed us with Your Son

Put forth precepts that are holy

Guided my actions to keep them holy

Granted the perfect example for me to follow to train my mind on things that are holy

HALLELUJAH

He is so awesome, So full of power and compassion

He reaches down and fulfills my every need in an amazingly expedient fashion

I don't even have time to wait or desire anything for long

He doesn't hesitate to show me that with Him is where I belong

Chorus

When I can't fathom His power increasing, I think, "He can't possibly show me more."

He instructs me to be obedient and turn the knob. And I behold another opened door.

FOUNDATION TO FINISHING

I may not have reached His Kingdom yet.

But as long as I can call the name of Jesus I'll have not one regret.

He promised there would be one that when He was gone would supply all things holy

Just as Moses, Abraham, Job, and the Disciples learned you can depend on God solely.

No matter the form of life; All Powerful Being, Man, or Holy Ghost.

It is his awesome power that controls all things

so no one man boast.

Chorus

CHORUS: He is so awesome. Hallelujah He reigns in me. Who am I to have the Power of the Living King inside of me.

GODFRIEND

Take me slow Lord; You know I'm not quick to follow.

I must investigate all angles and make sure there is not pitfall.

I know child, did you forget it was Me who made the call?

You're right, but I've been hurt so many times.

I try and I try but I always end up hurt.

I keep sifting to find gold but all I end up with is the dirt.

You know why that is, because that's all people are without Me.

Now I know- it took me awhile to figure that out.

And I found a church with some loving people to help teach me
what that was about.

I learned without You there is none good.

No matter the good qualities they've had.

The outcome without Jesus to guide me always turned out bad.

The bad may not have been clear at first it may have taken a long time.

But a life without Jesus has no hope of salvation

And those men are not going to be a long-term relation.

The men who follow Christ are far from perfect.

But at least we'll have something in common, where we can always return.

Because the flames that are ignited by Christ are much safer to let burn.

Yes, Lord I'll follow you especially to the selection of my mate.

Who else knows the heart so thoroughly, all the hidden places.

You know me I get caught up with just the handsome faces.

FROM GOD WITH LOVE

The road you are taking is yours and yours alone

Whether you make a right turn or a left

The path you are following is for you

Keep seeking and you will find

Just what the King wants for you

You may not know what lies ahead

But rest in the knowledge that it was tailor made for you

Only a loving God would hold your hand And even carry you if
needed

Because He knows His thoughts of you and His plans for you

His love is abounding and seeks nothing in return

That is depicted by the sacrifice He made of His Son for you

A preparation is needed; to get your mind, soul and body in line

If this is not done you will not receive all the spiritual things

He has promised in His Word for you

FREE

It has taken me awhile and I'm still not sure how

I wasn't simply down

I was most definitely out

But He gave me a way. Out of no way.

And on this day I am FREE

Been tossed to and fro

Didn't know where to go

Surely someone can tell me the way. Can anybody tell me which way to turn?

I looked high and I looked low.

And He showed me the way. Out of no way. And on this day I am FREE.

It was crystal clear. I should have had nothing to fear.

The path was straight and narrow but not many make it here.

But He pointed out the way. Out of no way. And on this day I'm FREE.

CHORUS

There was darkness and I felt there was no one on my side.

But in His wings I decided to hide.

Of course there were those who said He's not going to want you.

All Glory to God those people had no clue.

Those fools were blocking the way, controlling the gate.

Filled with no love just judgment and hate.

And He still made a way. Out of no way. And on this day I'm FREE.

CHORUS

Jesus my King. This all consuming fire. Burning me up making sure He's my only desire.

Lord of Lords. My Prince of Peace. He was there when all the world was at a cease.

The Breath of Life. The Living Water the flows and washes away all strife.

The Kingdom is near and man still doesn't know the way. But I proclaim to you on this day.

That He will show you the way. Out of no way. And on this day you too can be FREE.

CHORUS: Free to live. All I have to give. This life is a gift. He gave it to me to serve Him in truth. Don't let another day go by before you tell the devil he's a liar. To live in love and truth is your command because the Hour is at hand.

LAST CHORUS: Free to live. All you have to give. This life is a gift. He gave it to you to serve Him in truth. Don't let another day go by before you tell the devil he's a liar. To live in love and truth is your command because the Hour is at hand.

DON'T PUSH

I heard you say you don't want to push Me on anybody If you don't tell them how are they supposed to know?

Didn't I lovingly persuade you to believe in Me?

How can you not want My popularity to grow?

Entire generations are dying because of lack of knowledge

And you say you don't want to push Christ the Savior on anyone

Don't push. Just mention My name

Or do you think by dropping My name it'll ruin the fun

You talk about everyone else you love and spend time with

Am I not special enough for you to give the slightest recognition?

I'm not asking you to speak volumes upon volumes of all that I am

I just ask that you testify to the reason for your eternal position.

You know; your place in heaven which I have secured for you You do know there is room enough for all who wish to enter

I wouldn't know that you are aware of that fact because you're not increasing my Kingdom

Since you have made the vow not to push What are you...a Christ dissenter?

When I called you that included certain responsibilities on your behalf

Praise, prayer, spreading the gospel and making disciples to name a few

Is that too much to ask?

I hope not My love; but remember when you feel like you're going to push...I am always here with you.

AWE

God, You are so awesome

The depth of Your love for those who believe

God Almighty it is unsurpassed

There are those who wonder what I have that makes me so joyful and at peace

I attempt to explain the greatness that is You But they can not fathom something so wonderful

God, You are awesome

The depth of Your love for those who believe

God Almighty is unsurpassed

Some question why I wait for You

They can't understand my complete and utter devotion to You But what I can't understand is Your complete and utter devotion to me

God, You are awesome

The depth of Your love for those who believe

God Almighty is unsurpassed

All I must do is cry out; plead for Your unmatchless grace and mercy And You serve it to me expeditiously A silent plea will also summon Your presence

God, You are so awesome

The depth of Your love for those who believe

God Almighty is unsurpassed

You're coming soon I know

You're preparing a place for us with the Father You're interceding for us even now

God, You are awesome

FOUNDATION TO FINISHING

The depth of Your love for those who believe

God Almighty is unsurpassed

BASES COVERED

Who's on first?

Jesus

What's on second?

Grace and mercy

I don't know who's on third.

The Holy Spirit, don't you know He's there?

Who's on first?

Jehovah

What's on second?

Everlasting peace

don't know who's on third.

Do you want to know?

Who's on first?

FOUNDATION TO FINISHING

God Almighty

What's on second?

Unspeakable joy

I don't know who's on third.

Who do you want to be there?

Who's on first?

The Comforter

What's on second?

Healing

I don't know who's on third.

Did you ask?

Who's on first?

My redeemer

What's on second?

Cleansing for my soul

I don't know who's on third.

Don't you?